# CLEMENTINE ROSE

## and the Paris Puzzle

# Books by Jacqueline Harvey

*Clementine Rose and the Surprise Visitor*
*Clementine Rose and the Pet Day Disaster*
*Clementine Rose and the Perfect Present*
*Clementine Rose and the Farm Fiasco*
*Clementine Rose and the Seaside Escape*
*Clementine Rose and the Treasure Box*
*Clementine Rose and the Famous Friend*
*Clementine Rose and the Ballet Break-In*
*Clementine Rose and the Movie Magic*
*Clementine Rose and the Birthday Emergency*
*Clementine Rose and the Special Promise*

*Alice-Miranda at School*
*Alice-Miranda on Holiday*
*Alice-Miranda Takes the Lead*
*Alice-Miranda at Sea*
*Alice-Miranda in New York*
*Alice-Miranda Shows the Way*
*Alice-Miranda in Paris*
*Alice-Miranda Shines Bright*
*Alice-Miranda in Japan*
*Alice-Miranda at Camp*
*Alice-Miranda at the Palace*
*Alice-Miranda in the Alps*
*Alice-Miranda to the Rescue*

# CLEMENTINE ROSE
## and the Paris Puzzle

# Jacqueline Harvey

RANDOM HOUSE AUSTRALIA

A Random House book
Published by Penguin Random House Australia Pty Ltd
Level 3, 100 Pacific Highway, North Sydney NSW 2060
www.penguin.com.au

Penguin
Random House
Australia

First published by Random House Australia in 2016

Addresses for the Penguin Random House group of companies can be
found at global.penguinrandomhouse.com/offices.

National Library of Australia
Cataloguing-in-Publication Entry

Author: Jacqueline Harvey
Title: Clementine Rose and the Paris puzzle/Jacqueline Harvey
ISBN: 978 0 85798 788 4 (pbk)
Series: Harvey, Jacqueline. Clementine Rose; 12
Target audience: For primary school age
Subjects: Girls – Juvenile fiction.
        Paris (France) – Juvenile fiction.
Dewey number: A823.4

Cover and internal illustrations by J.Yi
Cover design and additional illustration by Leanne Beattie
Internal design by Midland Typesetters, Australia
Typeset in ITC Century 12.5/19 by Midland Typesetters, Australia
Printed in Australia by Griffin Press, an accredited ISO AS/NZS
14001:2004 Environmental Management System printer

Penguin Random House Australia uses papers that are natural, renewable
and recyclable products and made from wood grown in sustainable forests.
The logging and manufacturing processes are expected to conform to the
environmental regulations of the country of origin.

*For Ian, just because*

# PARIS

Clementine's eyes were the size of dinner plates as she knelt up onto her seat and pressed her nose against the glass. Her breath fogged a tiny patch of window.

'Look!' she called, pointing to the street as their minivan came to a stop.

Lady Clarissa craned her neck to see what her daughter was excited about this time. Clementine hadn't stopped talking since they'd arrived in the city, exclaiming about something every few seconds. Will scanned left and right as he tried to keep up with the little girl's pronouncements.

'That's Notre Dame Cathedral,' Clementine's Great-Aunt Violet said. 'I was married there, actually.'

'I didn't know that,' Clarissa said. She looked over at Digby Pertwhistle, who shrugged his shoulders in reply.

'Might we enquire what number wedding that was?' he asked cheekily.

Violet Appleby's top lip curled. 'No, you may not.'

'I've been there before,' Will piped up. 'It's got the best windows.'

'Perhaps we should all go tomorrow,' Aunt Violet suggested.

Clementine shook her head. 'I was pointing to the dog, not the church.'

Sure enough, a tan-coloured beast that looked more lion than canine was waiting patiently by the roadside. It sported a matching navy coat and lead while its owner had a well-trimmed beard and wore a beige safari suit. A trilby hat was perched atop the man's head at just the right jaunty angle. Together, owner and hound made quite the stylish pair.

Will gasped. 'He's ginormous!'

'He's huge, all right,' Digby agreed. 'I wouldn't like to pay his food bills.'

'Or clean up his messages,' Drew added.

Clementine wrinkled her nose, and Lavender grunted as if to agree. The little pig was sitting on Digby's lap, looking out the window too.

'I think we're almost there,' Drew said. He knew Paris well, having visited many times for work.

The minivan turned left and puttered along a winding cobblestoned street before crossing a main road that was brimming with colourful shops and restaurants.

'Look at those heavenly flowers,' Aunt Violet sighed longingly. The pavement outside a florist was bursting with blooms. 'We could gather some ideas for the wedding, Clarissa, and perhaps even pick out a dress.'

'Who are you marrying this time?' Uncle Digby quipped, unable to help himself.

Aunt Violet pretended she hadn't heard him.

Clementine turned from the window. 'I thought Mrs Mogg was going to make your dress, Mummy,' she said.

'Good grief, I think we can do better than that,' Violet Appleby tutted. 'Fancy coming all the way to Paris and not taking advantage of the chic boutiques. *I'll* most certainly be doing some shopping while we're here.'

'Did you discover a money tree before we left home, Miss Appleby?' Digby Pertwhistle looked at Clementine and winked.

'Modelling pays quite well, I'll have you know,' Aunt Violet said importantly. 'In fact, Elaine told me that her friend Rodolphe, who owns a fabulous boutique here in Paris, said I would have been perfect for one of his shows. It's just a pity they were held last week.'

'Does this Rodolphe have a red nose, by any chance?' Uncle Digby asked.

Clementine and Will dissolved into a fit of giggles.

Violet Appleby shot the butler a dark look. 'Rodolphe has a very handsome nose. Elaine showed me a photograph and I thought he looked like a movie star.'

'Maybe he'll fall in love with you, Aunt Violet, and then you can stay in Paris and get married in Notre Dame again,' Clementine said.

Digby nodded. 'And live happily ever after in the bell tower.'

Aunt Violet tightened her lips like the drawstring on a bag, but for once she decided to bite her tongue.

The minivan pulled up to a pair of ornate iron gates. Everyone spilled out and followed Drew into a courtyard crowded with flowerpots and hanging baskets brimming with red geraniums.

Clementine looked up at the pretty white townhouse. She thought it was lovely, though it was much smaller than Penberthy House. 'Mummy, can we go to the Eiffel Tower?' she asked. She had spotted the famous structure in the distance on their way to the city and was desperate to go right to the very top.

'It's a bit late, darling,' Clarissa replied. 'I think we'll just have time to eat dinner and get settled in.'

'But we're only here for a week and I want to see *everything*,' Clementine protested.

Drew turned to her and grinned. 'Everything?'

Clementine nodded emphatically. *'Oui, monsieur.* Everything.'

Clarissa Appleby smiled and shook her head. 'Come along, then. We'd best get a move on.'

# L'HÔTEL LULU

A tall, thickset man with glasses greeted the group as they entered the hotel foyer. He wore a natty grey waistcoat and a white shirt with the sleeves rolled up. '*Bonjour*,' he declared with a grin.

Clementine's tummy fluttered ever so slightly at the prospect of speaking French to a real French person. '*Bonjour monsieur*,' she replied quietly.

The man leaned forward, his eyes sparkling. 'And what is your name?'

'I'm Clementine Rose Appleby and –'

'But of course!' he said, throwing his hands into the air. 'You are the competition winners.'

The door behind the reception desk opened, followed by the sound of skittering claws. 'Lulu, come back here at once,' a woman called.

But the little dog was on a mission and raced out to greet their guests. Within seconds the miniature dachshund and the teacup pig were nose to nose, matching one another sniff for sniff.

A woman wearing a short skirt and a pink silk blouse emerged from the doorway and scurried after the copper-coloured dog. Her brown hair was piled in loose curls on top of her head. *'Bonjour,'* she said. 'I must apologise for that naughty creature. The minute she hears new guests she is in such a hurry to say hello.'

Lulu was now licking Lavender's snout while the tiny pig danced around, squealing. It almost sounded as if she were giggling.

'You are the people with the petite piggy!' the French woman exclaimed. Lavender

snuffled at the lady's feet, then nuzzled against her leg. 'Oh my goodness, what an adorable creature.'

'She likes you,' Clementine said, as she and Will knelt down to give Lulu a pat.

'She is *magnifique*,' the woman replied, cradling Lavender like a baby and kissing her nose. 'We have never had a piggy stay in the hotel before. She has such wonderful manners, perhaps she will teach Lulu to share. My husband's dog is the most spoiled creature you will ever meet.'

'That is not true, Camille,' said the Frenchman. He walked out and scratched Lavender's head before picking up the dachshund. 'Please allow me to introduce myself. I am Henri Crabbe and this is my wife, Camille, and my beloved Lulu. It is our great pleasure to welcome you to our hotel.'

'Thank you so much for accommodating Lavender,' Clarissa said. 'I wasn't sure if you'd take a pig but I thought it wouldn't do any harm to ask.'

'We are delighted to have her with us. She reminded me so much of Capucine,' Camille replied.

Clementine was surprised. No one had ever told her that Lavender reminded her of coffee before. 'Really?' she asked.

'She is famous. Come, I will show you.' Camille hurried to the cabinet behind the counter and pointed to a photograph of a woman wearing a fur coat and a matching hat. She had ruby-red lips and heavily made-up eyes and she looked to be dangling a papier-mâché pig on long strings.

Aunt Violet peered at the picture. 'Is that a marionette?'

'*Oui*,' the woman replied. 'That is Capucine. She is the most famous pig in Paris and probably all of France.'

'But she's a puppet,' Will said.

'Who's the woman holding her?' Uncle Digby asked.

'Madame Delacroix, the most famous puppeteer in the country,' said Monsieur

Crabbe, 'or at least she was when I was a boy. I suspect Capucine's fame is waning these days. There is a theatre in the Luxembourg Garden, where I think she still performs. It was always a wonderful show.'

Drew nodded. 'That sounds great. We should take a look.'

'We must let you go upstairs and rest,' Henri said, handing Clarissa the keys. 'Your rooms are all on the second floor. Breakfast is served in the basement restaurant, which is also open for dinner.'

'And if you need anyone to look after Lavender while you are here, I will happily volunteer,' Camille added.

'Thank you,' Clementine said, then quickly covered her mouth with her hand. 'Oops, I meant to say *merci*.' She peered up at the woman. 'Do you know my friend Sophie?'

'Don't be ridiculous, Clementine,' Aunt Violet scoffed. 'Do you have any idea how many French girls are called Sophie? There must be a million in Paris alone.'

'Her father is Pierre and her mother is Odette and she has a brother called Jules,' Clementine continued, undeterred.

Camille Crabbe's eyes lit up. 'Why, Pierre is our baker! He is running his papa's patisserie just around the corner. It is very sad that Monsieur Rousseau is unwell at the minute, but to tell you the truth, I think he is more lonely than ill.'

Clementine could barely contain her excitement. 'Have you met Sophie? We're seeing her tomorrow.'

'*Oui*,' Madame Crabbe replied, 'but she did not mention that you were coming to visit.'

'It's a surprise,' Clementine said proudly. 'Mummy said it would be more fun that way.'

Madame Crabbe nodded. 'Sophie will be very excited. I think she will be leaping out of her lizard skins.'

Clementine's brow furrowed. She didn't recall Sophie's skin ever resembling anything like that of a lizard. She wondered what could have happened.

Henri Crabbe snorted. 'You are mixing your metaphors again, my dear. Sophie might be leaping like a lizard or jumping out of her skin, but she is certainly not leaping out of her lizard skins.'

Clementine looked at Will and the pair of them giggled into their hands.

Camille Crabbe's face flushed. 'I think I need to go back to my English classes.'

'Come along, everyone,' Drew said as Henri Crabbe and Uncle Digby loaded the family's bags onto a silver luggage trolley.

Clementine spied a rack of leaflets on the wall near the elevator. 'There's the Eiffel Tower and the glass pyramid and a palace,' she said, nudging Will and pointing to the display.

Madame Crabbe collected a few of the brochures as well as a small map. 'You will need these for your explorations,' she said, holding them out to the children.

'*Merci*,' Clementine replied, taking them from the woman. 'There are so many things to see!'

'If you are lucky, you may also see snow tomorrow,' Madame Crabbe said.

'Snow!' Clementine gasped. 'Imagine the Eiffel Tower all covered in white – that would be like a dream.'

Clarissa smiled. 'You'd better get to bed straight after dinner, darling. Maybe then your dreams will come true.'

Clementine's face lit up. 'I hope so,' she said, jiggling up and down excitedly. The lift bell sounded and she and Will dashed inside.

# BONJOUR

Clementine's eyes fluttered open. For a moment she wondered where she was. Then a thought as gentle as a feather settling upon a pillow came to her and she remembered she was in Paris. She pushed aside the bedcovers and tiptoed to the window, careful not to wake her mother. Clementine pulled back the curtain and peered into the dark street. There was still no sign of snow. Her fingers danced along the freezing glass as she hoped for it to come later in the day.

There was a rustle and then the sound of Lavender's trotters on the floor. Clementine felt the little pig's snout tickle the back of her leg. She turned and pressed her finger to her lips. 'Shh. Don't wake Mummy up.'

Clementine reached down and took the creature into her arms.

'Sophie is somewhere out there,' she whispered. 'Do you think she's missed me too?'

Clementine shivered, but not from the cold. She glanced around at the wingback armchair in the corner of the room, where her mother had laid out her clothes for the day. She put Lavender on the chair and began to get dressed, taking extra care not to poke any holes in her new tights, just like Aunt Violet had taught her. When she was ready, she helped Lavender into her very own red coat.

'Good morning, darling,' Clarissa yawned, sitting up in bed. 'You two have made an early start.'

'I'm so excited, Mummy. I can't wait to see Sophie,' Clementine said. She placed a matching red beret on Lavender's head and tickled the pig under the chin.

'Me too,' Clarissa said. She hopped out of bed and gave her daughter a hug.

Clementine looked up at her mother. 'There's still no snow,' she said.

'You mustn't be too disappointed, sweetheart,' Clarissa said, cupping Clementine's face with her hands. I don't think it's a particularly regular occurrence in Paris.'

Clementine pouted at the ground. 'I'll keep wishing because you never know.'

While Clarissa got ready, Clementine spread her map across the floor. She ran her finger over all of the places she and Will had circled the night before. Lavender sniffed the Arc de Triomphe.

It wasn't long before Clarissa was dressed too. As she finished doing up the buttons on Clementine's new red coat, which Mrs Mogg had made especially for the trip, a knock sounded on the connecting door to their suite.

'*Entrez*,' Clarissa trilled.

Drew poked his head in and smiled. 'Ready?'

Clarissa nodded.

Drew glanced around. 'Where's Clemmie?'

'I'm right here,' Clementine said, skipping over to him.

'But you're not Clementine,' he said, a row of frown lines crisscrossing his forehead. 'Aren't you a little French girl?'

Clementine's face split into a grin. 'No, silly, it's me. It must be the beret that tricked you.'

'*Oui*, it is superb!' he said with a thick French accent.

Will walked through the adjoining door, dressed in a white shirt with a beige jacket over the top. He chuckled at the sight of Lavender. 'It's the piggy from Pa-ree.'

'I think she looks beautiful,' Clementine said.

Will nodded. 'You look really nice too,' he said with a smile.

'*Merci*,' Clementine said in her best French accent.

'*De rien*,' the boy replied.

'Listen to you two,' Clarissa said, shaking her head in wonder. 'You'll be mistaken for locals.'

'Do you think so, Mummy?' Clementine asked hopefully.

'I can't wait to learn some more words,' Will said.

'From real French people too,' Clementine added with a nod. The children had been practising every day before the trip, endeavouring to master as many French words and phrases as they could.

'Well, there's no time like the present. Your real-life French class awaits,' Drew said. He offered Clarissa his arm and, together, they ushered the children and Lavender out the door.

## A MISHAP

After a hot breakfast, the group of seven bundled out into the cold and set off for Pierre's father's patisserie. Clementine insisted on consulting the map, so Drew helped her to trace the route with her finger and they discovered that it wasn't far at all. They just had to turn the corner, walk past a row of townhouses and through a small square.

Clementine loved the way the chairs and tables at the front of the cafes faced outwards in a long line as if to watch a fashion parade go by. There were lots of people rugged up in coats, scarves and gloves, sipping from steaming cups. In the middle of the square, two boys raced around an old iron fountain, flicking the icy water at one another, much to the annoyance of their grandmother.

'The patisserie should be down there,' Drew said, pointing to an avenue of shops on their left.

Clementine caught sight of a sign that looked a lot like the one for Pierre's shop back home. Except this patisserie's name started with an 'E'. Clementine sounded it out. 'E-t-i-e-n-n-e-s. Etienne's Patisserie.'

'Well done, darling,' Clarissa said. 'That's the name of Sophie's grandfather.'

The butterflies in Clementine's stomach were doing backflips and somersaults and leapfrogs and pirouettes all at the same time. She quickly passed Lavender's lead to Uncle Digby and began to run.

'Slow down, Clementine,' Aunt Violet warned.

Just as the child reached the door, it swung open and a woman barrelled outside, balancing a tower of cake boxes in her arms.

'Look out!' Clarissa called, but it was too late.

The tower teetered back and forth before toppling to the ground in an avalanche. The topmost box burst open, splattering a large creamy cake all over the footpath.

'Oh no!' Clementine cried, cradling her face in her hands.

'*Zut alors!*' the woman bellowed. Her face was the colour of overripe tomatoes and her jet-black hair seemed charged with static electricity.

Clementine stared at the mess in front of her and began to feel very hot despite the cold weather. 'I'm s-s-sorry,' she stammered, as Lady Clarissa and Uncle Digby raced over to help.

Clementine felt terrible. She had been so excited to see Sophie and now she'd ruined everything. Tears spilled onto her cheeks.

'It's all right,' Drew said, giving her a reassuring squeeze. 'It was an accident.'

The woman marched towards Clementine, jabbing her finger at her. 'What were you thinking, you silly little girl? Children like you should be locked up!'

'Don't you speak to my great-niece like that,' Aunt Violet barked. 'It was hardly intentional, and children should most certainly *not* be locked up for bumping into old women who carry more than they are capable of managing.'

The angry woman's eyes narrowed. 'If I am old, then you are positively one foot in Père Lachaise!'

Aunt Violet's mouth fell open. Clementine had no idea what that place was but she guessed it wasn't anywhere good.

'What did that lady say?' Will whispered to his father.

'She said Aunt Violet has one foot in the grave,' Drew whispered back.

Digby Pertwhistle scooped up Lavender and cradled the pig inside his coat. He didn't want the woman to have another thing to complain about and, given half a chance, Lavender would have happily hoovered the remains of the cake from the ground.

Clarissa began to pick up the boxes. The first cake was well and truly mangled but the other three looked as if they could be saved.

'That was the last caramel sponge,' the woman sniffed loudly. 'And caramel sponge is my favourite.'

Clementine wiped the tears from her eyes and took in the cranky woman's fur coat and the slash of bright red lipstick across her pouty lips. There was something about her that seemed oddly familiar. It suddenly dawned on Clementine that she looked a lot like the lady in the picture Madame Crabbe had shown them yesterday.

'Please, *madame*,' Clarissa said, 'come inside and I will arrange another cake for you.'

'I do not have time. You have made me very late,' the woman snapped. She grabbed the boxes from Clarissa's hands and was about to storm off when Clementine found her voice.

'Are you the lady with the puppets?' she asked.

The woman turned and stared at her. 'What did you say?'

'Madame Crabbe showed us a photograph of a lady who looked a lot like you. She had a pig called Capucine,' Clementine explained. She was pleased with herself for remembering the name of the puppet.

The woman raised her nose in the air. 'Do you mean Camille Crabbe, the ditsy woman who chased me all over St Germain with her camera?'

Clementine shrugged. 'I guess so. Madame Crabbe said that you're the most famous puppeteer in all of Paris.'

'What rot!' the woman scoffed. 'I am the most famous puppeteer in all of *France*.'

Clementine shrank into Aunt Violet's side. 'That's what I meant to say.'

Drew seized the opportunity to introduce himself and the others. 'We were hoping to take the children to see your show,' he said warmly. 'Monsieur Crabbe recommended it. He says you are magnificent.'

'Did he now?' The woman batted her false eyelashes. 'It seems Monsieur Crabbe has impeccable taste. I am Paulette Delacroix.' Just as she spoke, Lavender poked her head out of Uncle Digby's coat. Madame Delacroix's brow wrinkled, resembling three rows of purl stitching. 'You have a *porcelet*?' she gasped.

Clementine wondered what that was. She knew that the French word for pig was *cochon*.

'No, she's a *mini cochon*,' Aunt Violet said curtly. She still hadn't forgiven the woman for the remark about being one foot in the grave, nor her appalling behaviour towards Clementine.

Paulette Delacroix shook her head in disbelief. 'I have never heard of such a thing.'

'Madame Delacroix, is that Capucine?' a man called out from a cafe across the road.

Everyone turned to find a small crowd of onlookers had begun to gather there.

'Isn't she adorable?' Madame Delacroix called back. She dropped her cake boxes and snatched Lavender from Digby's arms.

Several people approached and asked if they could have their photographs taken with the famous puppeteer and her star.

'Please, one at a time,' she said, and smiled as Lavender squirmed to get away.

'Madame Delacroix, allow me to get you another cake,' Clarissa insisted.

The woman waved a hand at her. 'Don't be ridiculous. It was just a silly accident. I must be more careful in future. I was, after all, carrying far too much,' she said, shooting Aunt Violet a smug look. 'You can repay me by bringing your lovely little piggy to the show on Friday.'

'Just Lavender?' Uncle Digby asked.

'Oh, of course not. You must all come, especially the dear children,' Madame Delacroix gushed.

She passed Lavender to Clementine and picked up her parcels, ignoring the pleas of several more passers-by who were keen to have their photographs taken with her.

'I have to go but you must all come to my show.' She blew kisses to her adoring audience and disappeared down the cobblestoned lane beside the patisserie, leaving Clementine and her family wondering what on earth had just happened.

# REUNION

Drew held open the door as everyone filed inside. The bell tinkled just the way it did at Pierre's shop in Highton Mill and the familiar smell of freshly baked bread and cinnamon filled the air. Clementine closed her eyes and breathed it in, the corners of her mouth lifting into a smile.

A slim woman with short blonde curls greeted the group. Clementine looked around, her stomach sinking when she realised that Pierre wasn't there and neither was Sophie.

Just as she feared the worst, a cheerful figure wearing a white apron and a baker's hat appeared from the back of the shop. Clementine ran towards him and leapt into his outstretched arms.

'*Bonjour, ma chérie!* Now, that is the best cuddle I 'ave 'ad all day,' the man said as Clementine kissed his left cheek and then his right. 'You 'ave turned into a little French girl, Clementine.'

She smiled as Pierre returned her to the floor and greeted the rest of the group. Last of all, he knelt down and gave Lavender a scratch under the chin.

''Ow is my favourite piggy?' he asked, and Lavender grunted in reply.

Clementine eyed the doorway to the back of the shop. 'Where's Sophie?'

'She is at 'ome with Odette and Jules,' Pierre replied. Spotting her disappointment, he quickly added, 'I did not want to spoil your big surprise. We will be there in mere minutes, I promise.'

Clementine smiled, relieved to hear it.

Pierre introduced them all to his helper, Emmanuelle, then hung up his hat and apron and ushered the group out onto the street.

'Enjoy your reunion,' Emmanuelle called, farewelling them with a wave.

The others waved back, promising to return another time for treats.

They walked to the end of the row of shops, then turned into a narrow cobblestoned lane. A pretty iron gate covered in ivy blocked their path. Pierre pushed it open into a courtyard lined with hanging baskets and pots of neatly trimmed box hedges. A three-storey townhouse with tall French doors on the ground floor and Juliet balconies above filled the space.

Will and Clementine raced ahead to the front door. Clementine could feel the excitement rising in her whole body. She looked at Pierre expectantly as he stepped onto the porch beside her. He gave her a wink and buzzed the front doorbell.

There was the sound of rushing feet, thudding louder and louder until coming to an abrupt stop at the door.

'Who is it?' a girl asked from the other side.

'Just open it,' a boy could be heard whining.

Pierre nodded at Clementine, who looked fit to burst. 'It's me!' she called.

The lock clicked and the door swung open to reveal Jules and Sophie Rousseau. Jules' jaw dropped in disbelief while the two girls squealed and rushed into each other's arms.

'What are you doing here?' Sophie demanded.

Odette appeared with a sly grin on her face. 'It is so good to see you all,' she said, wiping a tear from her eye.

'I've missed you so much,' Clementine said to her best friend.

'Me too,' Sophie replied, with an extra-big squeeze. 'Sorry, I just had to check that you were real.'

While the adults greeted one another and spoke of adult things, the girls shot off inside with Lavender, Jules and Will hot on their heels.

# HIDE AND SEEK

Clementine left Lavender in the Rousseaus' large eat-in kitchen, where she quickly made herself known to Pierre's father's cat, a grumpy calico creature named Hortense. The puss didn't seem the least bit pleased with the visitors and she certainly wasn't interested in Lavender's attempts to play.

Sophie and Jules showed off their rooms upstairs and the group was about to head back to the kitchen when a creak sounded overhead, followed by a dull thud.

Will looked at Jules. 'What was that?'

'Do you have a ghost?' Clementine asked. Unlike most children her age, she didn't mind the idea of ghosts at all, especially as she liked to imagine her own grandparents floating around Penberthy House in the evenings.

'It's just Grand-père,' Sophie said, turning her eyes to the ceiling.

Clementine gasped. 'Did he die?'

'No, silly, he's not a ghost,' Jules said.

'What's he doing up there?' Clementine asked. She loved exploring the attic at home and always managed to find some interesting thing she'd never seen before.

'Remembering,' Sophie said.

Clementine nodded. 'Sometimes I forget things too, like where I put my toy snake, but I think it gets worse when people get older. Aunt Violet always says she doesn't remember how to use the washing machine.'

'Is he feeling better?' Will asked.

'It's hard to tell,' Jules said, toeing a pull in the carpet. 'He doesn't have a cough or a runny nose and he hasn't been in hospital since we got here but –'

'He spends most of his time in the attic,' Sophie said. 'When I went to ask if he was coming down for dinner yesterday he was just sitting there, staring at an old book. It was as if he couldn't hear. I had to say his name three times.'

'Can we meet him?' Clementine asked. 'Maybe he could become friends with Uncle Digby and Aunt Violet. They're old too.'

Jules looked at his sister. 'Let's say hello. But hold your nose – it smells like wet socks up there.'

The children followed Jules to the end of the hallway, where he opened what looked to be a cupboard door. Inside, there was a winding staircase similar to the one at Penberthy House but much smaller. They thumped their way upstairs into the vast space, which was crisscrossed with dusty oak beams.

'Grand-père,' Sophie called, but there was no answer.

They emerged into a huge room filled with all manner of household cast-offs. Clementine spotted suitcases, a hat stand, old cupboards and chests of drawers. Unlike Penberthy House, there were no ancient taxidermied animals like Theodore the warthog, at least upon first inspection.

A shuffling sound led the children to the far end of the space, where an old man with a thick head of silver hair was hunched over a box, sorting through a pile of something or other.

'What are you doing, Grand-père?' Sophie asked, touching him gently on the elbow.

Startled, the man turned around suddenly as if only just registering that the children were there. 'Oh, nothing important,' he said, waving a black-and-white photograph in the air. 'What brings you up here, *ma chérie*?'

'I thought you'd like to meet our guests,' Sophie replied. 'Clemmie is my best friend from home and Will is going to be her brother soon, when their mum and dad get married.

They came to visit and it was a big surprise, but maybe you knew that already.'

'Ah, perhaps your mother did mention it the other day. *Bonjour*,' the man said, with the slightest hint of a smile.

'*Bonjour*,' Clementine and Will echoed shyly.

'Are you feeling better, Monsieur Rousseau?' Clementine asked. She was hopeful that he was on the mend so that Sophie could return to Highton Mill. She hadn't had a chance to tell her all about awful Saskia Baker and the trouble she was causing at school. The sooner Sophie could come home, the better as far as Clementine was concerned.

'*Comme ci, comme ça.* I have good days and bad,' the old man said. He stared at the picture in his hand and his thick caterpillar eyebrows furrowed.

Clementine's face fell.

'Who's that in the photograph?' Sophie asked.

Her grandfather handed it to her. 'That is me when I was a boy and that was my best friend, Solene. We lived in the same village in Provence.'

'Where is she now?' Jules asked.

'I do not know. I moved to Paris, and when I returned to visit my family a few months later, I heard that she had eloped,' the man explained. 'Her parents did not approve of the marriage and never spoke of her again.'

'That's so sad,' Clementine said. She couldn't imagine never speaking to her mother again.

'She was clever. She made beautiful things,' the man said, smiling to himself.

'What sort of things?' Sophie asked.

Before her grandfather had time to reply, Odette's voice filtered up from the bottom of the attic stairs. 'Morning tea is ready. I made 'ot chocolate,' the woman called.

'Yum!' Sophie exclaimed.

'Do you want to come and have something to eat, Grand-père?' Jules asked. 'There's caramel eclairs.'

The old man patted his stomach. 'I do not think I need any more pastries, Jules. I will stay here a while longer.'

The children bid farewell and barrelled down the stairs, all the while talking of garden adventures and rescuing Lavender from horrible Hortense.

Clementine up-ended the bowl and allowed the soggy marshmallow to slide into her mouth. 'That was the best hot chocolate I've ever tasted,' she declared.

Odette had made traditional *chocolat chaud*, which Clementine and Will had first mistaken for soup because of the way it was served in bowls instead of mugs. The children had lapped at the warm milk like kittens while Aunt Violet regaled the Rousseaus with the story of Madame Delacroix.

Lavender had given up on Hortense and was sitting under Uncle Digby's chair, enjoying the titbits he was feeding her. The calico cat was lazing by the range, preening herself and shooting the pig dirty looks.

Odette took the saucepan from the stove and topped up the children's bowls with the last of the hot chocolate.

'So you 'ave met my most famous customer,' Pierre said to Clementine.

The child nodded. 'I don't think she likes me very much.'

'Oh, 'er bark is worse than 'er bite,' the man said. 'We should all go to 'er show. Per'aps I will take 'er some caramel sponge cake.'

'Madame Delacroix 'as been famous since I was a girl,' Odette said. 'Or I should say that Capucine 'as been. She used to 'ave 'er own television show.'

'Well, I found the woman appalling,' Aunt Violet chimed in. 'I won't be going. I'd rather wash my smalls.'

The children snorted into their bowls and Jules almost spat out his drink.

'Do you mean your underwear, Aunt Violet?' Clementine said with a giggle.

The old woman nodded. 'I'll do yours too if it means I don't have to go.'

'Oh, wonderful,' Uncle Digby said, reaching for a cream bun. 'We won't have to wash when we get home, then.'

Aunt Violet shot the man a frosty look. 'I certainly won't be touching yours, Pertwhistle.'

Clarissa ignored the elderly pair and turned to Pierre. 'Did you grow up here?' she asked.

Pierre nodded. 'We moved to this 'ouse when I was a young boy. It is a beautiful place, although I think it is too big for my father to live in alone.'

Sophie ate the last bite of her caramel eclair and pushed back her chair. 'We're going to play in the garden,' she announced.

'Put on your coats,' Odette said.

Clementine bent down and picked up the little pig. 'Come on, lazybones.'

The children scampered out the back door, across the terrace, down a flight of steps and onto the lawn. Compared to Clementine's house, the garden was compact, but it had beautiful trees and hedges and a neat lawn.

'What about a game of hide and seek?' Jules asked.

There was a cloudy chorus of agreement as the children breathed out into the cold air.

'I'll be in first,' the boy offered. He stood on the bottom step and began to count aloud.

Will spotted a large stone pot and crouched behind it while Sophie shielded herself with a trellis covered in a leafy vine. Clementine scanned the yard for the perfect hiding place. As Jules reached five, she and Lavender ran to a thick bush at the bottom of the garden and squeezed in behind it. Lavender loved playing hide and seek at home and was very good at staying still until they were found.

'Ready or not, here I come!' Jules shouted.

Clementine held her breath.

Jules ran into the garden, his footsteps thudding on the grass. 'I can see you, Will,' he called.

Clementine peered out from the bushes just in time to see Will make a dash for home. She watched as Jules lunged at the boy and missed.

46

'Safe!' Will called out gleefully.

'Who's next?' Jules shouted, swivelling around. 'Where are you, Sophie?' he called in a singsong voice.

Clementine could feel her blood pulsing. She looked at her feet and discovered that the little pig had disappeared. 'Lavender,' she whispered, glancing around, 'where are you?'

'Gotcha!' Jules yelled, bursting through the bushes.

Clementine screamed and shot out, racing to get home before Jules could catch her, but he was too fast. Jules tapped her on the back and Clementine stopped, letting out a loud sigh. Her heart was thumping.

Sophie emerged from her hiding place. 'You're in, Clemmie.'

'Did you see Lavender?' Clementine asked, expecting to find the tiny pig charging about somewhere in the garden.

Jules shook his head.

'Don't worry, she can't get out,' Sophie said. 'The wall goes all the way around.'

'Lavender!' Clementine called. 'She likes being in with me.'

The children set off in different directions to try to find her. After they'd searched for several minutes with no success, Clementine began to worry.

'That's strange,' Sophie said, biting her lip.

'Maybe she's under a bush,' Will suggested.

Clementine ran back to her hiding spot, calling Lavender's name. It was then that she came upon an opening in the wall, where an old iron grate had fallen out. The others gathered around and peered at it in puzzlement. Clementine lowered herself flat onto the ground and began to wriggle through the hole.

'What are you doing?' Sophie asked in alarm. 'You don't know where that goes.'

'Exactly!' Clementine called back. 'I've got to find Lavender. She doesn't know anywhere in Paris.' The child's legs disappeared.

Jules was on his tummy next, pulling himself along on his elbows.

'What's over there?' Will called.

Jules gasped. 'Wow! It looks like an enchanted forest.'

That was all the encouragement Will needed. He quickly wriggled through the opening in the wall, followed by a reluctant Sophie.

# THE WITCH

The children's mouths gaped open as they stared up at the house. It looked like something from one of the not-so-nice fairytales. Surrounded by a border of thick hedges and an army of knobbly trees with twisted roots, it rose up from the ground three storeys high. Clementine's eyes widened as she took in the large covered terrace on the ground floor and the open balcony above, accessed by two pairs of curved French doors. The third floor was set into the gabled roof with intricate

50

windows and ornate timber work, although all of it had seen better days. Shutters with flaky paint hung at skewed angles from broken hinges and several roof slates were cracked with a couple missing altogether. But even in its sad state, the house was beautiful.

'What is this place?' Clementine puffed.

'Do you think anyone lives here?' Will whispered.

'A witch,' Sophie said, her voice wavering. 'Or maybe you'll find your ghosts after all, Clemmie.'

'Look, there are faces in the windows!' Will gasped, although he couldn't see them clearly through the grimy glass.

'I don't think they're real,' Jules said.

'Lavender!' Clementine called out. She worried for her pet, who was probably feeling a bit scared by now, all alone in the overgrown garden.

Sophie put a finger to her lips. 'Shh!'

'But I have to find her,' Clementine said, charging through the dense foliage.

After a moment's hesitation, the others followed. Sophie felt the hairs rise on the back of her neck as they neared the house. She looked at the window set into the top of the back door and stopped in her tracks. 'W-w-what's that?' she stammered.

A clown's head was nodding and its hand was waving as if to say hello.

'Stop!' Sophie pleaded. 'The house *is* haunted.'

'It's just a puppet,' Jules said. 'Don't be such a baby!'

Will hung back beside Sophie, who was shaking all over and not just from the cold. The boy took her hand and she held onto him tightly.

Inside the house, the woman was surprised to hear the high-pitched sound of children's voices getting louder. It didn't usually take much more than a dancing clown to be rid of them. In fact, she hadn't seen a child out there for years now, not since a lad had run away screaming about a witch. It wasn't that she had an aversion to youngsters, she just found them bothersome. She wondered where this lot had come from and what they were doing in her garden.

A loud squeal sounded, causing the woman to drop the puppet in her hands. The noise did not belong to anything human – she was sure of it. She pulled aside the curtain on the back door and was stunned to find a tiny pig wearing a red coat.

A blonde child in a matching coat raced onto the terrace and scooped the little creature into her arms. The girl looked up and, spotting her, smiled. The woman recoiled, dropping the curtain and pressing her back to the wall.

She swallowed hard as the child knocked loudly on the door.

# MADAME JOUBERT

Clementine stood on her tippy-toes and tried to see in through the lace curtain. She wondered why the lady didn't open the door. 'Hello?'

Lavender nuzzled Clementine's cheek.

'Did you make a new friend?' she asked the little pig. Clementine knocked again but there was no reply.

Just as she was about to give up, the door opened ever so slightly. Clementine and Lavender peered into the room. An old woman with white hair pulled back into a neat bun was standing just inside. Her clothes were splattered with paint and Clementine noticed that her hands were too.

'*Bonjour*,' Clementine said. 'I just wanted to apologise for Lavender wandering into your garden. We were playing hide and seek,' she explained, motioning to her friends. Jules and Will were standing just off the terrace but Sophie had positioned herself further away under a pear tree, ready to make a speedy escape. 'Lavender must have come in through the hole in the wall between Monsieur Rousseau's garden and yours.'

The woman's brow wrinkled and she gazed over Clementine's shoulder. She didn't know her neighbour but there was something familiar about that name.

'I'm Clementine Rose Appleby,' the child offered. The old woman hesitated.

'She probably doesn't speak English,' Jules said.

'Clemmie, we have to go home,' Sophie called out.

'I am Madame Joubert,' the woman said. Her voice was hoarse, as if she hadn't used it in a very long time.

'That's a lovely French name,' Clementine said, then realised how silly she sounded. 'I suppose that's because you're French, of course.' She giggled. 'These are my friends Sophie and Jules and that's Will,' she said, pointing at the taller boy.

The woman stared at the group, a bewildered look on her face. Lavender grunted and wriggled in Clementine's arms.

'Sorry to have bothered you, Madame Joubert,' Clementine said finally, and turned to leave.

'May I see your *cochon*?' the old woman asked, opening the door a little wider.

Delighted, Clementine turned back and stepped closer to the threshold. 'You can hold her if you like.'

Madame Joubert retreated and shook her head.

'At least give her a pat. She doesn't bite but

she might lick you,' Clementine warned. 'She's always tickling my fingers.'

The timid woman was mesmerised by the miniature beast. Slowly, she reached out and touched Lavender's bristly head. As she made contact, she pulled her hand away sharply and gasped.

'Don't be scared,' Clementine said.

Madame Joubert placed her hand back on Lavender's head and this time she left it there, gently stroking the creature. Lavender leaned her snout towards the woman and licked her fingers.

'*Incroyable*,' the woman said, a faint smile playing on her lips. 'She is very beautiful.'

Suddenly, a voice cut through the still air. 'Jules! Sophie!' Pierre called. 'Come out, come out wherever you are!'

Madame Joubert gasped and retreated behind the door.

'It's all right,' Clementine said. 'That's just Pierre. He must think we're still playing hide and seek.'

She was about to say goodbye when she noticed the clown marionette lying in a tangle on the floor.

'Is that a puppet?' Clementine asked. She looked further into the room and saw there were lots of puppets. They were hanging from high cupboards, from the backs of chairs and even from the range. There were princesses in beautiful gowns, animals of all shapes and sizes, jesters and jugglers, clowns and witches.

The woman nodded.

'We're going to a puppet show,' Clementine told her. 'The star is a little pig called Capucine. She looks just like Lavender.'

Madame Joubert's eyes narrowed and a fierce look clouded her face. '*Non!*' she snapped and, to Clementine's great surprise, slammed the door.

Clementine blinked. She wondered what she had said wrong. Paris was such a lovely place but she didn't understand why all the old ladies were so cross.

The children wriggled back through the opening in the wall and into Monsieur Rousseau's tidy garden. Clementine felt as though they'd stepped out of the pages of a fairytale and back into real life.

Pierre watched the children reappear one by one from the bottom of the garden – Jules with dirty trouser knees and Sophie's face a ghostly white. Will's beige coat was smattered with leaves while Clementine, carrying Lavender in her arms, seemed to be sprouting twigs from her beret.

'Where 'ave you lot been?' he asked.

'Sorry, Papa. Lavender escaped into the neighbour's yard,' Jules explained. 'There's a hole in the bottom of the wall where a grate has fallen out.'

Pierre's eyebrows lifted in surprise. 'You are braver than me. When I was a boy, my friends and I were terrified of the witch next door.

Let me tell you, we lost many footballs to 'er garden. Legend 'ad it that you didn't go into that garden because you might never come out again.'

Sophie shivered. 'I told you that house was haunted.'

'Come along,' Pierre said. 'Odette and your parents 'ave made plans to do some sight-seeing, and I must get to work or else poor Emmanuelle will think I 'ave abandoned 'er.'

'I hope we're going to the Eiffel Tower,' Clementine said as the children charged up the steps and into the warm house, soon forgetting all about the strange old lady on the other side of the garden wall.

## OFF WE GO

T he group of family and friends wandered
along past a boulevard of shops, taking
their time to have a proper look around.
They were on their way to visit Notre Dame
Cathedral and the Louvre, which Clementine
and Will had circled on the map as places they
wanted to see. Clarissa had promised they
would visit the Eiffel Tower tomorrow or the
next day, when they had more time.

Clementine loved looking in all the windows
and trying to work out what each of the shops

sold. Outside one of them, a pungent odour much like that of sweaty socks thwacked her in the nose.

Clementine pinched her nostrils and tried to read the sign on the window. 'From-a-ger-ie. What's that?'

Sophie smiled. 'It's a cheese shop and they have the stinkiest, mouldiest cheese in the world,' she replied.

'A whole shop just for cheese?' Clementine's eyes widened. 'That's amazing.'

'No, that's delicious,' Aunt Violet interjected.

They moved on to the next shop, which left Clementine completely confused. 'Why is there a shop for poison?' she asked.

Sophie shook her head. 'They sell fish.'

Clementine reeled. 'Do people eat poisonous fish in France?'

Jules overheard the conversation and chuckled. 'Not on purpose. It's *poisson*, with a *pwah* sound, not poison. It means fish.'

'Oh.' Clementine sighed with relief as she gazed at the buckets full of slimy sea creatures.

Will pulled a face. 'They stink too,' he said, hurrying away.

As they passed Etienne's Patisserie, Pierre waved at them through the window. The group stopped to wave back, then continued down onto Boulevard St Germain towards the Latin Quarter. Traffic buzzed along the streets and there were lots of people walking around too.

Clementine felt a warm shiver run through her bones. It was so exciting to be in Paris. 'Do you like living here?' she asked Sophie.

Her friend frowned. 'It's fun but school is hard. Even though Jules and I speak French, it's different to Ellery Prep,' she explained. 'I can't understand some of my teachers very well.'

'Is there anyone like Mrs Bottomley?' Clementine asked. After meeting Madame Delacroix and Madame Joubert, she thought her Kindergarten teacher would fit right in with the cranky old ladies of Paris.

Sophie nodded. 'Madame Marceau. I think she's even meaner than Mrs Bottomley but she wears nicer clothes.'

'It's a lot different at school without you,' Clementine said.

'What's the new girl like?' Sophie asked.

'Mummy says she's challenging but Aunt Violet says she's despicable,' Clementine said, then launched into a long explanation of what had happened at their barbecue and the school Grandparents' Day. 'Her father can't make cream buns the same way your dad does either,' she added.

'That's horrible. I hope we can come home soon,' Sophie said, squeezing Clementine's hand.

'Me too,' Clementine agreed. 'You have to be back in time for the wedding. It wouldn't be the same without you there.'

Just as Clementine mentioned the wedding, the group walked past the most beautiful bridal salon she had ever seen. Inside, sparkling crystal chandeliers glinted against the polished woodwork. A sign with swirly writing hung above the doorway.

'Mummy, look at that,' Clementine gasped.

Clarissa stopped and turned to see what her daughter was admiring this time. In the window was a breathtaking gown. It had a delicate lace bodice and full tulle skirt.

'It's a lovely dress,' Clarissa said, her cheeks flushed, 'but I'm far too old to wear anything like that.'

'Nonsense,' Aunt Violet scolded. 'It's your wedding, Clarissa, and you should wear exactly what you want and be as extravagant as you like. You're only going to get married once.'

'What sort of dress did you have, Aunt Violet?' Clementine asked.

'I think you mean *dresses*, Clemmie,' Uncle Digby added cheekily.

Aunt Violet glared at the man. 'Oh, do be quiet, Pertwhistle. At least someone wanted to marry me. I haven't exactly noticed a queue for your hand.'

Digby Pertwhistle's face fell and Clementine couldn't work out if he was play-acting or if Aunt Violet had really hurt his feelings this time.

'I'm sure there are lots of ladies who would love to marry you,' Clementine said quietly.

'It's all right, sweetheart,' Uncle Digby replied. 'Somewhere out there, the woman of my dreams is missing out on an expert washer-upperer and silver polisher.'

Clementine slipped her hand into his. 'You're really good at making beds too.'

The adults grinned.

'Come on, everyone. We've got plenty of time to sort out my dress when we get home,' Clarissa said, eager to move on.

Soon enough, the group found themselves wandering along the river Seine, and in the distance they could see the enormous cathedral. As they crossed a narrow bridge, the children were stunned to find thousands of padlocks attached to the side railings.

'What are they for?' Clementine asked.

'They are love locks,' Odette replied. 'Couples write their names on them and attach them to the bridge as a symbol of their eternal love. The problem is, they are causing the bridges to come apart. They've already taken down the locks from the Pont des Arts because it was in danger of collapsing under all that weight.'

'It's a bit silly,' Will said. 'People don't need a lock to prove they love each other.'

Drew wrapped an arm around Clarissa and kissed her on the cheek. 'I couldn't agree more.'

'There's the Eiffel Tower!' Clementine yelled, peering over the rail and pointing. 'Please can we go today?'

'Tomorrow, Clemmie,' her mother replied. 'I promise.'

Clementine sighed. She wondered if they'd ever get there.

'Let's take some photographs, shall we?' Drew pulled the lens cap off his camera. 'How about one of your modelling poses, Aunt Violet?'

The old woman smiled. 'I suppose. We are in Paris after all.' She spun around with her hand on her hip and pouted like a professional.

# SIGHTSEEING

The Rousseaus and their guests visited Notre Dame Cathedral, where the stained-glass windows were every bit as spectacular as Will had said.

'Eight hundred years old!' Clementine exclaimed, her voice echoing around the cavernous building. 'But that's even older than our house, Uncle Digby.'

A stern-looking lady shushed her, wagging a finger crossly.

Clementine clamped her hand over her mouth. 'Sorry,' she whispered.

'Keep your voice down, Clemmie. We are in church, you know,' Aunt Violet admonished, only to have the stern woman give her the hairy eyeball too.

After a while, they emerged, blinking into the sunlight. The group then strolled down the other side of the river, towards the Louvre. By now it was well past midday and the children's stomachs were grumbling.

They found a cafe along the river that had an enclosed front veranda, where several people were sitting with their dogs. The man at the front desk didn't seem to mind that Lavender was more of a pig than a pup and was happy for them to take a table at the end of the restaurant. Lavender caused quite a stir and a few people wandered over to pat her. Clementine got the distinct impression that pigs weren't a regular sight on the streets of Paris, with one man even offering to buy the tiny creature on the spot.

After devouring their delicious lunch of lemon-and-sugar crepes, the group made their way to the Louvre. Clementine and her friends raced over to the huge glass pyramid and leaned against the structure, gazing down into the art museum.

'Look, you can see all the people walking inside,' Will said, pointing at the tops of the tourists' heads.

'Why is the museum under the ground?' Clementine asked.

Sophie shrugged. 'I'm not sure but there are lots of things under the ground in Paris – like the Métro.'

'Is that the train system?' Clementine said. She remembered how Drew had pointed out some of the staircases leading down to the stations along the way.

'And the catacombs,' Jules said, wriggling his eyebrows.

'What's that?' Clementine asked as her eyes tracked a lady wearing a large fluffy hat down below.

'Tunnels with skeletons,' Jules answered in a whispery voice.

Odette shot her son a warning look. 'Jules, do not scare the girls.'

Clementine's eyes widened. 'Are they real?'

Jules checked to see that Odette wasn't watching before he nodded.

Clementine felt a thrill of excitement run down her spine. 'Can we go?' she asked her mother.

'We can ride on the Métro, but we might give the catacombs a miss,' Clarissa said firmly. 'My parents took me when I was little and I had nightmares for months.'

'I wouldn't have bad dreams,' Clementine said. There was an old medical skeleton in the attic at Penberthy House that she quite enjoyed playing with. Clementine looked over at the entrance and noticed a few people standing outside with dogs, but none of them were going in. 'Do we have to leave Lavender outside too?' she asked.

Odette bit her lip. 'Oh, dear me, I 'ad forgotten. There are no pets allowed inside any of the museums or galleries.'

'I can take her,' Aunt Violet offered. 'I've been to the Louvre more times than I can count and I wouldn't mind doing a spot of shopping.'

'I'll come with you,' Uncle Digby said. 'It won't be easy fending off all the admirers you're likely to encounter along the way.'

Aunt Violet blushed. 'I can handle myself perfectly well, Pertwhistle.'

'I meant the hordes who will be admiring *Lavender*,' Uncle Digby said.

The old woman's blush deepened. 'I knew that,' she snapped.

Clementine passed Lavender's lead to Uncle Digby and gave the pig a big hug before the trio set off.

The museum was crowded with an assortment of visitors. There were tour groups and elderly couples, as well as young artistic-looking individuals with flamboyant clothes and over-sized sketchpads. Several people had their noses so close to the paintings you'd have thought they were able to smell them, not just see them.

Clementine craned her neck to catch a glimpse of a small portrait hanging on the wall. It seemed that everyone else in the museum had come to view it too. Just as she was about to weave her way through the forest of legs to get a better look, Drew scooped her up onto his shoulders.

'There you go, Clemmie,' he said. 'What can you see?'

Clementine studied the famous painting. 'I can see a lady sitting down very quietly,' she replied. 'Do you think she has a secret?'

'Maybe,' Drew said. 'Many people wonder what she's smiling about.'

'I think she looks like she's got wind and she blamed the cat for it,' Jules said with a snicker.

Clementine wrinkled her nose. 'There's no cat in the painting.'

Will began to laugh, and the old man standing beside them got a fit of the giggles too.

'What is it with boys and bottoms?' Odette tutted, shaking her head.

Clementine tilted her head to one side and considered the painting for a while longer. 'I think she might be in love,' she concluded.

'Yes, that's a much better idea,' Drew agreed, chuckling to himself. 'Now, how about we take a look at the sculptures?'

Clementine thought about how many more rooms there might be. The museum seemed positively enormous and she was tired. 'Can we go home?' she asked. 'I'm 'sausted.'

Will, Sophie and Jules all nodded in support.

'I don't want to look at all those naked bodies again,' Sophie added. 'Mama and Papa took us there when we first arrived in Paris and it was *so* embarrassing.'

'I've got an idea,' Odette said to Clarissa. 'Why don't I take the children 'ome so you and Drew can 'ave some more time to explore? We might go to the Luxembourg Garden on the way and the children can 'ave a turn sailing boats on the pond.'

'Yes!' the kids hissed, pumping their fists.

It was settled. The children headed off with Odette, while Drew and Clarissa wandered towards the sculpture gallery.

# AHOY!

The children charged through the garden gate with renewed energy. 'Can we go to the pond?' Jules asked, trying to remember which way it was.

Clementine's blue eyes were huge as she took it all in. 'There's a palace!' she exclaimed. 'Does a princess live there?'

'Not anymore,' Jules said. 'There was a big fight and all the royal people in France lost their heads.'

Clementine's jaw dropped. 'Is that true?' she said.

Odette nodded. 'I am afraid it is, but it was a long time ago when the ordinary people were very poor and the royal family was very rich and they didn't care about their subjects.'

Clementine scrunched up her face. Mr Smee always told their class that violence never solved anything, and chopping off heads was the worst thing she'd ever heard of.

'The pond is this way,' Jules shouted. He grabbed Clementine's hand and they charged off with Will and Sophie close behind.

They ran to the elderly man and his fleet of little antique model sailboats. Clementine chose a boat with a red sail, while Sophie opted for a blue-and-white one. Jules pointed to a green sail, and Will decided he would have a pirate sail with a skull and crossbones emblazoned across it.

The man handed them to the children as well as a long stick to launch their sailboats. 'I would advise you to take them to the other side so the breeze will send them back across,' he said.

They did as he suggested. Although the sun was shining, the afternoon air was crisp and the children almost had the duck pond to themselves. They discarded their gloves and, with numb fingers, placed their boats onto the icy water in a neat row.

'On your marks, get set, go!' Odette called, and the foursome pushed out their sailboats.

'Go, red boat,' Clementine shouted, urging her vessel on.

The boats darted across each other's bows, at the mercy of the breeze. At one point the pirate ship almost crashed into Jules' green sailboat. The children cheered and raced about all over the place in an effort to follow their vessels, pushing them out again when they veered too close to the edge.

As she watched the sailboats glide around the pond, Clementine thought about the places they had seen. Paris, she decided, was the most beautiful city in the world. The buildings were all so elegant and the people were too. Some of the boutiques even had guards stationed

at their doors. Aunt Violet had said that the clothes in those shops cost a lot more than a car or even a house. Clementine had started to wonder if many Parisians had jobs, though, as the streets and cafes were always full of people drinking coffee and hot chocolate.

'Who won?' Odette asked as the last vessel was scooped from the water.

'We all did, except for Sophie,' Jules said. 'Her boat kept going around in circles.'

'It was a stupid boat,' the girl griped.

The group bade farewell to the old man with the sailboats and headed to the gate on Boulevard Saint-Michel. Odette walked ahead with Jules and Will while Sophie and Clementine straggled behind, stopping to look at something every minute or so.

Clementine was admiring another pond with a grand fountain when she caught sight of a lady wrapped up in a fur coat and sunglasses striding towards them. She wore bright red lipstick and was holding a large carry bag. The child smiled and waved.

'*Bonjour* Madame Delacroix,' she called, running over to her.

The woman stared at Clementine as if she had just stepped in something unpleasant.

'It's me, Clementine, from the patisserie,' the child reminded her.

Madame Delacroix pushed her sunglasses to the top of her head. 'Oh, yes, how could I forget? The cake destroyer. But where is your *cochon*?' she asked.

'Lavender had to go home because museums don't like pigs,' Clementine said. 'It's silly because I know she would have loved all the paintings.'

'But you will bring her to my show?' the woman asked with concern. 'I have the television people coming and they are going to do a *huge* story on me and my puppets. Little Lavender will be a great help to me.'

Clementine grinned and nodded. 'Lavender is like that. She helps me with my homework all the time and she loves to listen when I tell her poems.' Her eyes drifted to the woman's bag and she noticed a timber cross and some strings poking out of it. 'Is that a puppet in there?' she asked.

Madame Delacroix's lips pursed. 'She is broken, and without her my show simply cannot go on.'

'Is it Capucine?' Clementine asked, trying to take a peek.

The woman clutched the bag closer. '*Oui*, but I must go. Bring your *cochon* to my show on Friday morning and do not be late,' she demanded, then stormed away down the path.

Clementine hurried over to the gate where the group was waiting.

'Who was that you were talking to?' Odette asked. She bent down and straightened Clementine's beret.

'Madame Delacroix,' Clementine replied. 'She owns the puppet theatre.'

She thought about Madame Joubert and her many puppets, and decided to pay her another visit. Maybe she had a spare piggy she could lend to Madame Delacroix.

# AN UNEXPECTED ADVENTURE

The next day the family and friends visited another art gallery, which Clementine thought had much lovelier paintings than the Louvre. Her favourites were by a man whose name she had forgotten and she admired the scenes of his garden and the three ladies in a boat. The one she liked best of all was of a lady holding a parasol and standing with a boy in a field of red poppies. It was beautiful.

'Are we ever going to the Eiffel Tower?' Clementine sighed as they left the gallery.

'Well, you'll just have to wait and see,' Drew said as the family set off once again.

It wasn't long until Clementine looked up and the structure was looming over them. 'We're here!' she squealed, jumping up and down on the spot. 'And it's *enormous*!'

The children raced around the bottom of the tower while the adults queued for the elevator. Once inside, Clementine pressed her face against the glass, not wanting to miss a thing. The lift sped to the first level, where they changed to another lift that would take them all the way to the top. The view was just as spectacular as Clementine had hoped. She and Will spent quite a while pointing out all the different landmarks until their teeth chattered so much they could no longer speak.

Back on the ground, Clementine spotted a clown and wove her way through the crowd to stand right in front of the man. He wore a striped shirt and yellow pants with blue polka dots. His giant shoes were the largest Clementine had ever seen and she loved the way his rainbow-coloured hair stuck out in tufts from under his funny pork-pie hat. His red nose glowed as he produced another nose from his top pocket and handed it to Clementine. She giggled and put it on.

The clown then pulled a balloon from his ear and put it up to his mouth. He puffed and puffed but nothing happened. He waved at the crowd to help him. Clementine laughed as grown men and women puffed out their cheeks and mimed along with the clown. The crowd clapped and cheered until, finally, the clown blew his balloon into a long cylinder. Clementine watched as he twisted and pulled and, in no time at all, had created a balloon sausage dog.

'It's just like Lulu!' she exclaimed, as the clown passed her the creature.

Clementine turned around to show Sophie and was met with a sea of unfamiliar faces. Her breath caught in her throat and her heartbeat quickened when, all of a sudden, Aunt Violet surged through the crowd.

87

'Oh, thank heavens you're here!' the old woman said, grabbing Clementine in a bear hug. 'I thought we'd lost you.'

'I wasn't lost, Aunt Violet,' Clementine said. 'I knew exactly where I was, and I remembered what Mummy told me to do if I ever found myself on my own. I should stay in one spot until someone came, and here you are.' Clementine held up her gifts. 'The lovely clown made me a sausage dog and he gave me a red nose.'

Aunt Violet thanked the clown and threw some money into the man's open violin case. His eyes almost popped out of his head when he saw how much she'd given him. The clown quickly set about making Aunt Violet a bouquet of balloon flowers, which he promptly delivered with a sweeping bow.

Clementine couldn't stop smiling.

'So, was the Eiffel Tower as good as you'd hoped?' Aunt Violet asked.

Clementine grinned. 'It was even better.'

# DAY TRIP

On Wednesday afternoon the group made their way through the streets of Paris back to the hotel. They had spent the whole day at the Palace of Versailles, just outside the city. Lavender had stayed behind with Madame Crabbe as there were no pigs allowed at the palace, but she didn't seem to mind in the least. Lavender and Lulu were completely besotted with one another.

'Why didn't the king let the poor people live in the palace too?' Clementine asked her mother as they tripped along the street. 'There's plenty of room.'

'They were called peasants, Clemmie,' Aunt Violet interjected. 'I can hardly imagine that the king would have wanted his palace overrun with them. Could you imagine the smell?'

'But Mr Smee always tells us that it's better to share,' Sophie said.

'Exactly,' Will agreed.

'I think the king was being greedy and, anyway, they could have had a bath. There were plenty of bathrooms too,' Clementine said.

Drew and Clarissa looked at one another and laughed. 'It's nice to see the children have a well-developed sense of social justice,' Drew said with a grin.

'It was different back then,' Aunt Violet insisted. 'People were born to a particular class and you didn't get much choice about it.'

'Mummy says people can be anything they want to be, and France is probably a much better place since the peasants decided to eat cake,' Clementine said.

'What on earth are you talking about now, Clemmie?' Aunt Violet said, shaking her head. 'Queen Marie Antoinette famously said, "Let them eat cake", but she had no idea that the peasants couldn't afford it. She was being obnoxious.'

'Now everyone in Paris eats cake,' Clementine said. 'Look how busy Pierre is all the time. So it's much better these days.'

'We can have cake when we get home,' Jules said, nodding.

The children were looking forward to having a sleepover at the Rousseau residence that night. Drew had planned a special evening with Clarissa, including a surprise dinner at the restaurant at the top of the Eiffel Tower.

Once they arrived back at the hotel, Clementine waited in the foyer while her mother packed an overnight bag for her and Will. The others had gone ahead to the Rousseaus' to escape the cold.

'How did you enjoy the palace?' Monsieur Crabbe asked Clementine.

'It was very grand,' she replied, 'and there was lots of gold and mirrors everywhere. They must have really liked looking at themselves back then.'

Clementine went on to regale Monsieur Crabbe with her assessment of the French royal family and what she thought they should have done to prevent the revolution.

The man laughed heartily and nodded his head. 'Perhaps if we had Queen Clementine back then, we would not have had such terrible trouble.'

Clementine giggled as she imagined herself living in that enormous palace. 'I think being the queen might be a bit boring.'

Monsieur Crabbe agreed, and their conversation turned to what else Clementine had seen in the city.

It wasn't long before Lady Clarissa reappeared with a small suitcase, just as Madame Crabbe trotted into the hotel foyer with Lulu and Lavender.

'I am sorry but we have had so many admirers on our walk,' Camille puffed, passing

Lavender's lead to Clementine. 'I tell you, this little one will soon be the most beloved *cochon* in all of Paris.'

Clementine nodded. 'Madame Delacroix said Lavender will be on television when we take her to the puppet show.'

'Well, then you will have to fight off the fans with a stick,' the woman said.

'Lavender won't mind one bit,' Clementine said, picking up the little pig, who snuggled into her coat.

# PARIS PUZZLE

Odette cooked a delicious roast chicken dinner, complete with vegetables and gravy while Pierre had brought home a magnificent gateau for their dessert. Monsieur Rousseau joined them too, and he and Pierre talked a little about the patisserie. Pierre's father even said he would try to visit the shop for a few hours each day, which Clementine thought was a very good sign.

Meanwhile, Lavender had made herself at home in Hortense's basket by the range, which had seen the grumpy cat immediately decamp to a hiding spot somewhere else in the house. Lavender had no idea why Hortense didn't want to be her friend.

After dinner, Monsieur Rousseau vanished upstairs. Jules and Will cleared the table while the girls chatted about what they should all do before bedtime.

'We could play a game,' Clementine suggested, swinging her legs under her chair.

'Or you could do a puzzle,' Odette said, wiping the table. 'There's a lovely one in the attic. It's of a giant map of Paris.'

'That's a good idea,' Clementine agreed. 'We could use my map to help us.'

Pierre left the table to help the boys with the washing up and Odette disappeared to make up beds for their guests.

'We'll be back in a minute,' Sophie called as she and Clementine charged upstairs.

Clementine shivered as they entered the room. 'It's cold up here.'

'And Grand-père must have left the light on.'

Sophie led Clementine to the cupboard, where they found a pile of board games as well as the puzzle in its box. 'Shall we take a game too?' Sophie asked, shortly before a snuffling sound silenced the pair.

Sophie and Clementine looked at one another.

'Is that you, Grand-père?' Sophie asked.

The two girls headed to the other end of the room, where they found the old man sitting in a big armchair, with boxes of photographs scattered at his feet. His eyes were closed and his breathing was punctuated by little grunts.

'Shhh, he's asleep,' Clementine whispered.

'He can't stay up here. It's too cold.' Sophie looked around for a blanket to cover him with.

Etienne shuddered and the picture he was holding fluttered to the floor. Clementine picked it up and stared at the photograph of a young boy. The girl beside him looked to be about the same age and she was holding a puppet on a string. Clementine took a closer look at it and could see that it was, in fact, a marionette of a pig.

'I'll be back in a minute,' Sophie whispered. 'I'm going to fetch a blanket from downstairs.'

Clementine was about to put the photograph into one of the boxes when Monsieur Rousseau snorted and his eyes sprang open. She jumped back in fright.

The man smiled at her and straightened up in the chair. '*Bonjour* Clementine. Did I fall asleep again?'

Clementine nodded. 'You dropped this,' she said, handing him the photograph.

He yawned and stretched his neck, then focused on the picture. 'I am getting old,' he said. 'I spend too much time up here lately. Since Madame Rousseau . . .'

'Is that her?' Clementine asked, wondering if the man had known his wife when they were children.

'Oh no, that is my friend Solene,' he said. 'She was so clever – always making up stories. She made puppets too.'

'Really?' Clementine bit her lip. 'Did she make that one?'

'*Oui*. It was her favourite. A little piggy she called Capucine.'

'That's the name of Madame Delacroix's famous piggy,' Clementine said.

'Yes. When I first saw that *cochon* on television I thought it must have been Solene, but it turned out to be that mad woman who is all hair and lipstick.' Monsieur Rousseau grimaced. 'She comes into my patisserie all the time, always wanting things for free.'

'Why does she want things for free? She is famous all over France,' Clementine said.

'I think her riches have dwindled along with her fame. Children have so many enter-tainments these days,' the man said.

'It's funny that your friend and Madame Delacroix had the same idea about a pig called Capucine,' Clementine said.

A small smile perched on the man's lips. 'We used to put on shows in the village. My father helped us build a little stage on a cart and we would set up in the square and charge people one franc to watch.'

'I wonder what happened to your friend,' Clementine said, watching the man's face as he remembered.

'Life is a bit like a puzzle, *ma chérie*, and sometimes the pieces go missing,' the man said gently.

'The lady who lives on the other side of the back wall has lots of puppets in her house too,' Clementine said. 'I saw them.'

'The old witch who has let the place go to rack and ruin? I have never in my life set eyes on her, but my wife went to see her once when Pierre lost his football and came home in tears. My wife returned in tears too. That witch is not a nice lady.'

'I don't think she's a witch. I think she's just sad and lonely,' Clementine said, remembering how terrified the woman was of Lavender.

Footsteps thudded up the stairs and Sophie reappeared with a blanket in her arms. 'I brought this up for you, Grand-père,' she said.

'*Merci*, my dear, but I do not think I will stay up here tonight,' the man said, shifting forward in his seat. 'It is time to be with my family.'

'Would you like to help us with the puzzle?' Clementine asked. 'Aunt Violet and Uncle Digby sometimes help me with puzzles at home and they like to play games too. Aunt Violet pretends she doesn't but I know she does.'

'Why not?' The man nodded decisively. He smiled at the girls, then stood up and followed them downstairs.

Much to everyone's delight and surprise, Etienne spent the entire evening helping the children with their puzzle, and when their concentration wavered, he stunned them all with a rowdy game of charades.

# A DISCOVERY

Clementine and Sophie were making cupcakes in the kitchen while Will and Jules were busy building a model aeroplane. Rain thrummed against the window pane and thunder rumbled overhead. Clementine was ever-hopeful that the rain would turn to snow but Pierre said that it wasn't yet cold enough.

'I'm glad we're staying home today,' Clementine said. 'I think my legs are too tired to do any more walking.'

'Mine too,' Odette said as she placed the cupcake patties into the moulds. 'And it is good for your mother and Drew to 'ave some time to themselves, although it is a pity the weather is so bad.'

Clarissa had telephoned earlier in the morning to make plans, but Clementine and Will had both begged to spend the day at home with Sophie and Jules. Although Clarissa felt guilty for leaving the children with Odette, she conceded that they would probably prefer to be inside anyway. To everyone's astonishment, Aunt Violet and Uncle Digby had headed off to do some more sightseeing together, the old woman muttering something about lunch at a bistro in Pigalle.

'How is that mixture coming along?' Etienne asked, looking over at the girls. He was busy creating some sugar roses to put on top of the cupcakes.

'I think it's ready,' Sophie said, and switched off the mixer.

The old man walked over and dipped a finger into the bowl, then popped it into his mouth. *'Délicieux!'*

'Can we lick the beaters?' Sophie asked.

The man detached the silver stirrers from the machine. 'One for you,' he said, passing a beater to Clementine. 'And one for me,' he said, taking a big slurp of the gooey cake batter.

Sophie stamped her foot. 'Grand-père, that's not fair!'

'I am just teasing, little one.' He passed her the beater. Then, with the skill of someone who had done it a million times before, Etienne transferred the mixture into the patty pans and then placed them in the oven before the girls had finished their sticky treat. 'Odette, would you mind taking these out when they are ready? I think I should go and see what a mess that son of mine is making at the patisserie.'

Odette smiled. 'Of course, Papa.'

She was thrilled to see the old man so lively, and thought the children seemed to have the most wonderful way of bringing out the joy in him again.

'We'll do the washing up,' Clementine volunteered.

Sophie frowned at her. 'But I hate washing up.'

Clementine leaned in and whispered in her friend's ear. 'If your grandpa is better, then you can come home soon.'

Sophie nodded and raced to get the little footstool so she could stand at the sink.

'What are you up to?' Etienne said, raising an eyebrow.

Odette gave the girls a wink. 'They are just being good 'elpers, Papa.'

'What do you want to do now?' Sophie asked. It was well after lunch and the boys had gone back upstairs to work on their aeroplane.

Clementine and Sophie had made significant progress on their jigsaw puzzle of Paris but there seemed to be some pieces missing and they were feeling restless. Clementine had been thinking about Madame Joubert and wondered if she should ask to borrow one of her puppets for the show tomorrow. She looked outside and was pleased to see the sun was at last poking through the grey clouds.

'It's stopped raining,' Clementine said. 'Let's go outside.' She pulled on her red coat and wrapped a scarf around her neck. As she opened the back door, Lavender made a run for it.

'You should put Lavender on her lead,' Sophie said, as she wrestled with her jacket.

But Clementine had other ideas. She was hoping that Lavender might take another tour of Madame Joubert's garden.

Sophie stepped out to find Clementine dashing away. 'Come back,' she shouted, and gave chase.

Clementine peered through the hole in the wall.

Two deep frown lines traversed Sophie's brow. 'Did Lavender go through there again?'

'Yes,' Clementine replied. 'It's okay. I'll go and get her.'

'Not on your own,' Sophie said, hanging back. 'And the grass is wet. You'll get dirty.'

It was no use. Clementine had already squeezed through the opening. Sophie hesitated, not knowing what to do. She hopped on one foot and then the other. She really didn't want to go back into the witch's garden.

Meanwhile, Clementine could see Lavender snuffling around the base of a pear tree. She hurried over to the little pig and picked her up, then made her way to the house.

At that moment Madame Joubert looked out the kitchen window and was caught off-guard by the sight of a child heading for the back door. Her first instinct was to hurry away upstairs and pretend she wasn't home, but this time a little part of her wanted to know why the girl had returned, especially after she had behaved so badly the other day, slamming the door in her face.

'*Bonjour* Madame Joubert,' Clementine called, and knocked loudly.

The old woman sighed, more from habit than annoyance. She opened the back door. '*Bonjour*,' the woman replied quietly. 'Surely your *cochon* did not escape again?'

'Sort of,' Clementine said.

'There are truffles in my garden,' the woman said, 'and pigs love truffles.'

Clementine was surprised that the expensive chocolates Aunt Violet loved so much would be found in an overgrown garden. 'How many puppets do you have?'

'They are not your business,' Madame Joubert said curtly, her warmth evaporating.

'But you have so many of them,' Clementine said.

'Two thousand, seven hundred and thirty-one to be exact,' the woman mumbled.

Clementine's eyes widened in amazement. 'That's millions!'

Madame Joubert couldn't help but smile. 'Not quite, but I suppose it is a lot,' she admitted.

'Do you have any pigs? I thought I saw one in the kitchen the other day,' Clementine said, peering around the woman to get a better look.

Lavender squirmed and Clementine put her down to get a better grip. Without warning, the little creature shot off into the house.

'Lavender! Come back!' Clementine scampered after her, with Madame Joubert following close behind.

The creature ran up the stairs and along the hallway.

'Stop!' Clementine shouted.

'*Non!*' Madame Joubert called out.

Lavender sped on and turned into a room at the end of the passageway, where Clementine finally caught up to her. She scooped Lavender into her arms, then stood up and looked around the room. Clementine gasped. She couldn't believe her eyes. There were hundreds of marionettes and all of them pigs!

Madame Joubert stumbled into the room, huffing and blowing. 'Clementine,' she pleaded, 'you must not tell anyone.'

Clementine and Lavender reappeared through the hole in the wall to find Sophie waiting for them. The knees of Clementine's white tights were stained with mud and there were some dirty spots on her coat too. She was going to be in big trouble when Aunt Violet saw the state of her clothes.

'Did you see the witch?' Sophie asked.

'Madame Joubert is not a witch,' Clementine said. She was bursting to share her secret but the old woman had made her promise not to. 'Is your grandpa back?' Clementine asked. She had to talk to him as soon as she could.

'I don't know,' Sophie said, 'but your mother is here.'

Clementine looked at her knees and then at Lavender's muddy trotters. 'We'd better get cleaned up before she sees us.'

The three of them walked back to the house and made a beeline for the laundry room.

# BRAVO

Clementine checked again to make sure that Lavender was looking her very best. Mrs Mogg had made her a lovely striped top and red neckerchief, which she was wearing underneath her red coat. Clementine glanced around the theatre. There were rows of timber bench seats and a little stage at the front.

'I can't wait for the show to start,' Will said.

'I hope this thing doesn't go for very long,' Aunt Violet muttered as she sat down with a thud.

Madame Delacroix glided out from the side of the stage and strutted towards them. 'Quickly, give her to me,' the woman demanded. She snatched Lavender from Clementine's arms and whisked her away before anyone had time to reply. A cloud of her perfume descended upon the family.

Aunt Violet waved her hand in front of her nose. 'Pooh! That woman needs to learn the difference between a spritz and a shower. She must have emptied a whole bottle of scent over herself.'

'Will Lavender be all right, Mummy?' Clementine asked as she watched Madame Delacroix show her off to the television cameras.

Clarissa put an arm around her daughter and kissed the top of her head. 'She'll be fine, darling.' Clarissa would have much preferred the woman to include Clementine, but she contented herself with keeping a close eye on the proceedings.

Sophie and Jules soon arrived with their

parents, and Clementine was delighted to see Etienne with them too. The group shuffled to their seats in the front row.

As the room darkened, the spotlights shone on the stage, illuminating a painted backdrop of a farm. The music began and onto the stage waddled a fat farmer wearing overalls and a straw hat. Though he sang in French, Clementine recognised the tune to be 'Old MacDonald Had a Farm' and hummed along with it. Lavender sat by the side of the stage and, to the delight and fascination of patrons, grunted every now and again.

The audience was in stitches as the story progressed. With each scene came a new backdrop and a different animal – a horse, a duck, a lamb, a rooster and, last of all, Capucine dancing under the Eiffel Tower. Lavender loved it too and was jiggling about and squealing alongside the action. At the show's end, Madame Delacroix was basking in the glory. She dangled Capucine from one arm and held Lavender in the other.

'Bravo!' shouted a particularly enthusiastic man in the back row.

'We love you, Capucine!' another crowed.

Clementine jumped to her feet and clapped as loudly as she could.

Once the television crew had left and the newspaper reporters had snapped enough pictures, Madame Delacroix tottered over to the group with Lavender in tow. 'Your *cochon* is perfect,' the woman gushed. 'She is just what I need.'

'Lavender certainly looked to be enjoying all that fuss too,' Uncle Digby said. 'It's a shame we have to go home tomorrow afternoon.'

The woman gulped. 'You are leaving tomorrow? But you mustn't. There . . . there is still so much of Paris to see.'

'I'm afraid we have to,' Clarissa said. 'Clementine and Will have school, and we have guests booked into the hotel.'

'What are you doing in the morning?' Madame Delacroix asked.

'We're going on a cruise down the river,

but Madame Crabbe is looking after Lavender because we can't take her on the boat,' Clementine said.

'Oh, what a pity,' the woman replied, a smile spreading across her face. 'I'm sure you will still have a lovely time without her.'

# LAST DAY

As the boat pulled away from the dock, Clementine pressed her face against the window. The Paris skyline dazzled in the winter sunshine with the Eiffel Tower standing tallest among the grand buildings. It was all so beautiful – the bridges, the houses, the statues and monuments.

Clementine turned to her mother. 'Can we come back again?' she asked.

'Maybe one day,' Clarissa said with a smile.

'At least you've ticked off everything you and Will circled on your map.'

Clementine nodded. It had been a wonderful week. 'And more places too. Although it still hasn't snowed.'

'You never know,' Drew said. 'I might get to shoot a documentary here and we can live in Paris for a while.'

'But what would happen to Penberthy House?' Clementine said. She hated to think about them leaving their beloved home. Who would Granny and Grandpa have to talk to if she wasn't there?

'I'm sure Aunt Violet and Uncle Digby could manage the place,' Clarissa said, looking sideways at her aunt.

The old woman snorted. 'Godfathers, we'd likely kill each other in the first five minutes.'

But Uncle Digby didn't utter a word. He just reached over and patted Aunt Violet's hand.

Clementine expected him to get a slap on the wrist for his trouble, or at least a stern talking-to, but was surprised to see her great-aunt pat his arm right back. Clarissa and Drew grinned at one another as Clementine and the other children giggled.

'We're coming home soon,' Sophie said. 'So you can't leave.'

Clementine looked at her in surprise, unsure whether to cry or jump for joy. 'Really?'

'Grand-père is so much better. He says he wants to go back to work properly and he's even looking after the shop with Emmanuelle today,' Sophie said, smiling from ear to ear.

'I only wish 'e 'ad a companion,' Pierre said. He glanced at Uncle Digby and Aunt Violet. 'Like you two.'

'You know we can't stand each other,' Aunt Violet pointed out.

'I used to think that,' Pierre said, 'but lately I am not so certain.'

Clementine's tummy twinged as she remembered something she had meant to do. 'Will I get to see Monsieur Rousseau before we leave?' she asked.

'I don't know if there'll be time,' Clarissa said. 'We have to head off no later than four o'clock.'

Clementine frowned. She wished she was better at writing letters. That's what she would do as soon as she got home.

# AN INTERRUPTED FAREWELL

Clementine didn't want to say good-bye, but there was no choice in the matter. She hugged Sophie tight and then Jules. Odette brushed a tear from her eye as she farewelled her friends, and even Pierre smothered a sniffle or two.

'We will be back soon, I 'ope,' the man said with a smile. 'And definitely for the wedding.'

Amid a blather of tears, the Rousseaus parted company with the Applebys and Barnsleys.

Monsieur Crabbe was standing behind the

counter as the group trudged back into the hotel. 'My friends, what is the matter?' he asked, passing around a box of tissues.

Clarissa and Clementine wiped their eyes and Drew explained they were sad to be leaving their friends.

'Do not cry. I am sure you will be together again before long,' he said cheerfully.

Camille Crabbe walked out of the office. 'You are unhappy to be leaving us,' she said. 'Lavender will be sad too, I am sure.'

'Where is she?' Clementine asked. 'I need a hug from her.'

'She and Lulu are just through there.' Camille pointed at a door marked '*Privé*'. 'They were sitting in Lulu's basket watching my favourite game show when I left them.'

Camille Crabbe went to turn the handle and was surprised to find the door ajar. She pushed it open and looked inside. The television was on and Lulu was in her basket, but Lavender was nowhere to be seen. She saw the doors between the sitting room and the kitchen and bedroom were all firmly closed. 'Lavender,' she called.

'Why don't we finish packing?' Clarissa suggested. 'You can bring Lavender upstairs in a minute, Clemmie.'

'Yes, I think we're still in a bit of a mess, Will,' Drew added.

Clementine nodded. 'Okay.'

'I'll wait with her,' Uncle Digby said. 'I'm packed.'

Aunt Violet was momentarily distracted by the cover of a magazine on the corner of the reception desk. It featured none other than the famous designer Rodolphe, who, on second look, did seem to be in possession of a rather large red nose.

'Henri, can you come here, please?' Camille squeaked. Her voice was laced with an urgency neither Uncle Digby nor Aunt Violet missed.

'Is something the matter?' Digby asked as Henri disappeared through the door.

Clementine walked around the reception area, wondering what was taking so long, when the pair burst forth from the room.

'She is gone,' Camille blurted, wringing her hands.

'Who's gone?' Clementine asked, her bottom lip wobbling.

'Lavender,' the woman breathed.

Clementine whimpered. She could feel her heart racing but her head felt like it was full of cotton wool.

'Don't worry, sweetheart,' Uncle Digby soothed. 'Knowing our little busybody, she's just taken herself out for a walk.'

'I told you we should have left her at home,' Aunt Violet fretted. 'How will we ever find her now? The city is huge.'

Clementine glanced around the room through a haze of tears. She had no idea what to do. Her vision blurred before coming to focus on a fruit bowl on the reception desk and, in particular, a lovely ripe pear. Clementine blinked and wiped away her tears. 'I think I know where Lavender went,' she said suddenly.

'How could you possibly know that, Clementine?' Aunt Violet demanded.

'There's no time to explain. Aunt Violet, please call Pierre and tell him to look in Madame Joubert's garden,' Clementine said. 'Uncle Digby, come with me.'

'Not a chance. I'm coming with you too,' the old woman said, rushing to the front door.

'I'll telephone for you,' Henri said, without realising that he had no idea of the number.

Clementine, Uncle Digby and Aunt Violet sped along the street. Clementine urged them to go faster but they were both struggling to keep up. They ran as quickly as they could to the Rousseaus', only to find there was no one home.

Clementine rattled the gate, which was firmly locked. 'We can't get around the back to Madame Joubert's garden.'

'Slow down, Clemmie, or I'll have a heart attack,' Aunt Violet puffed.

'I'll be right behind you,' Uncle Digby wheezed, clutching at his chest.

'The shop!' Clementine yelled. They'd run straight past it, but Sophie's grandfather would still be there.

Forgetting about the last time she'd run full tilt towards the patisserie, Clementine charged back down the road to the shop. She pushed open the door and, fortunately, this time there was no one with an armful of boxes on their way out.

Etienne Rousseau looked up from where he was icing cupcakes. 'Clementine, what are you doing here?' he said.

'Lavender!' Clementine gasped, wincing from the stitch in her side. 'She's missing and I think I know where she's gone, but I need your help.'

The old man put down the icing bag and hurried over. 'Take a moment to catch your breath, *chérie*,' he said, as Emmanuelle quickly fetched the girl a glass of water.

'I think she's gone to Madame Joubert's garden,' Clementine hiccuped. 'Lavender can fit through the bars on your gate and then run through the hole in the wall.'

'What makes you think she is there?' the man asked.

'There are pears to eat and Madame Joubert said that she has truffles and pigs like them a lot,' Clementine explained.

Uncle Digby and Aunt Violet fell through the door of the shop, diverting Emmanuelle's attention. The pastry apprentice filled another glass of water and began fussing over the pair of them.

'All right, Clementine,' Etienne said, whipping off his apron and hat. 'But I know a faster way. We will go to her front door.'

Clementine suddenly remembered what she had been meaning to tell the old man the other day. 'Monsieur Rousseau, there's something you need to know about Madame Joubert,' she began.

'Later, *chérie*,' he replied, shrugging on his coat. 'We must find Lavender first.'

'We're coming too,' Aunt Violet said, and gulped down her glass of water.

The oddball group poured out of the patisserie and ran along the street with Etienne in the lead.

Clementine glanced at the man out of the corner of her eye, worried by his ragged breaths. 'Are you all right, Monsieur Rousseau?'

The old man thrust out his chest. 'I have not felt this alive in years!' he exclaimed.

Clementine grinned and looked ahead. 'That's it,' she said, pointing at the house that had a wall around the front of it.

She pushed open the lopsided gate and made her way through a stranglehold of vines. The house was just as dilapidated at the front as it was in the back and, if anything, the garden was even more overgrown. Clementine ran onto the front porch and pressed the bell again and again. She could hear it echoing through the house. By now Monsieur Rousseau, Uncle Digby and Aunt Violet were all standing behind her.

There was a shuffling sound and then, finally, the door creaked open just a tiny bit.

'It's me – Clementine,' the child blurted. 'I need your help, Madame Joubert. I think Lavender has run away into your garden.'

'What? Again? That pig must have a nose for truffles,' the old woman said. She swung open the door and was shocked to find that Clementine was not alone.

Clementine raced inside and through to the back garden, calling Lavender's name. Uncle Digby and Aunt Violet followed but Monsieur Rousseau was rooted to the spot. He gazed at the woman's face, tracing her features with his eyes.

'Solene?' he said at last.

Madame Joubert stared at the man's lined face and there was a glimmer of recognition. 'Etienne?' she whispered. 'Is it possible?'

Tears filled Monsieur Rousseau's eyes and spilled onto his cheeks as he looked at the woman who was once his best friend. 'I cannot believe it is you,' he said.

The pair embraced as if not a day had passed since they had last seen one another. Clementine and the others barrelled back through the house and to the front door.

'Lavender's not here,' Clementine said, and started to cry. 'What if we have to leave Paris without her?'

Madame Joubert released Monsieur Rousseau and stepped back. 'Where was she last?' the woman asked.

Clementine explained that Madame Crabbe had been looking after Lavender and Monsieur Crabbe's dachshund, Lulu.

Madame Joubert's brows furrowed. 'But the dog was still there?'

Clementine nodded.

'How curious,' the old woman said quietly. 'Perhaps someone has taken her?'

Clementine frowned. 'Why would anyone kidnap Lavender?'

'Come in and sit down,' Madame Joubert said, ushering the group into the kitchen. 'We must think.'

'I see you have not given up your puppets,' Etienne commented as they walked through the house. 'They are just as beautiful as I remember.'

Solene Joubert blushed and put on the kettle.

Clementine crawled onto Uncle Digby's lap, sniffling. He glanced at the newspaper sitting on the table when something caught his eye. It was a small photograph of Madame Delacroix and Lavender. He quickly turned to the story and pushed the paper towards Etienne. 'What does this say?'

Clementine looked over to see what he was talking about.

Sophie's grandfather quickly scanned the page. 'Capucine has come to life – Madame Delacroix is to launch a new show in spring at her world-famous puppet theatre,' he read aloud. 'It says that she is taking a break to develop a new show, and when she returns it will feature the real-life Capucine alongside her puppet friend.'

'She probably stole Lavender, just like she stole Capucine from me,' Madame Joubert said bitterly.

Everyone turned to look at the woman.

'What are you talking about, Solene?' Monsieur Rousseau demanded.

'It is too long a story for now,' the woman replied.

'Do you think Madame Delacroix could really have taken her?' Clementine asked, her eyes wide.

'I told you that woman was bad news,' Aunt Violet muttered.

Uncle Digby thought for a moment. 'Do you remember how she asked what we were doing this morning and where Lavender would be?'

Aunt Violet and Clementine looked at him as the same horrible conclusion dawned on them.

Madame Joubert thumped her fist on the table. 'She will not get away with this again. We must find her and rescue Lavender!'

# RED~HANDED

U ncle Digby ran out onto the road and hailed a taxi. The group piled into the vehicle and the car sped through the backstreets and across to the Luxembourg Garden. While Uncle Digby paid the driver, the others raced towards the puppet theatre.

The park was much busier than it had been on the days Clementine had visited. The motley group was forced to dodge and weave through people wandering about. Clementine arrived at the theatre first and tried the handle but the door was locked and there was a notice pinned to the middle of it.

Sophie's grandfather arrived next, his chest heaving.

'What does it say?' Clementine asked.

'Reopening on the first of March,' the man said, his face falling.

Huge tears began to trickle down Clementine's cheeks.

'Don't worry, Clementine, we will go to the police,' Etienne said, putting a hand on her shoulder. 'They will find our Lavender.'

Clementine's eyes widened and she pressed an ear to the door. She could have sworn she had heard grunting coming from the other side. 'Did you hear that?' she asked.

The old man jiggled the handle but it wouldn't budge.

'We are closed!' Madame Delacroix called from inside. 'Come back in spring for my new show.'

Aunt Violet and Solene Joubert finally reached the theatre with Uncle Digby in tow. But he wasn't the only one. They had come across two gendarmes in the park, who had listened eagerly to their fanciful tale.

'She's in there and so is Lavender,' Clementine said excitedly.

'Madame Delacroix, it is Officer Dufour and Officer LeBlanc,' said one of the policemen. 'Open up – we need to speak with you most urgently.'

There was a muffled noise from inside. 'I'll be there in a moment,' the woman's voice wavered.

'Hurry up, *madame*,' the officer ordered.

'Right, that's it then,' Uncle Digby said. He sized up the entranceway, took a few steps back and then ran towards it, executing a karate kick that sent him flying backwards, almost taking out Aunt Violet with him. He landed on the gravel with a thud. The doors rattled but remained locked.

'Godfathers, Pertwhistle! You're not a kung-fu master,' Aunt Violet said, running to his aid.

'*Madame*, open up at once,' the officer shouted.

'What if she is escaping out the back?' Monsieur Rousseau said.

The two young officers looked at one another before charging at the door, putting all their weight behind it. The wood splintered and the lock sprung open and there, with Lavender under one arm and a suitcase in the other, was Madame Delacroix.

'Lavender!' Clementine called. The little pig leapt from Madame Delacroix's grasp and raced into the girl's arms.

Solene Joubert stepped forward. 'Hello Paulette. Are you surprised to see me after all these years?'

Madame Delacroix's eyes almost popped out of her head at the sight of the woman, and she promptly fainted on the spot.

Just as Madame Delacroix was regaining consciousness, Clarissa, Drew and Will arrived on the scene, followed by the Rousseaus and

Camille Crabbe, who was clutching her hair and tottering along on her high heels.

'*Sacré bleu!*' she cried. 'Oh, thank heavens you found her.'

Clarissa hugged Clementine and Lavender. 'Darling, are you all right?'

Clementine nodded. She wasn't going to let Lavender out of her sight ever again.

Pierre looked at the old woman in the black dress and then at his father, who was standing beside her.

'Everyone, this is Madame Solene Joubert,' Clementine said, smiling at her new friend.

'She's the crazy lady who lives behind you, Grand-père,' Jules blurted.

'Solene?' Sophie gasped. 'Is she your friend from the village when you were a boy?'

'*Oui*, it is me,' Madame Joubert replied.

'But 'ow could you 'ave lived so close to us for all these years and not known?' Pierre said.

'I ran away from the village to get married a long time ago. My parents didn't approve but my husband was wonderful. We had a beautiful house and garden and I had a housekeeper called Paulette. She was my friend and she helped me with lots of things, and I taught her all about puppets. It was my dream to open a theatre and see my Capucine onstage,' the woman explained.

'And then what happened?' Sophie asked.

The entire group was hanging on Madame Joubert's every word. Even Officer LeBlanc had his notebook out and was furiously scribbling away.

'We were young and happy and full of dreams when my husband was killed in an accident. It was the worst day of my life. I could not cope and dear Paulette was so kind. Then one day, after months of feeling as if I was in a fog, I opened the newspaper and saw the article about Madame Delacroix's show. It was then that I realised Paulette had stolen Capucine and my idea for a puppet theatre.'

'But why didn't you tell the police?' Odette asked.

Camille Crabbe shook her head in disgust.

'She is a rotten thief. I am taking that woman's picture out of the cabinet and putting it into the rubbish as soon as I get back to the hotel.'

'Because I was weak and I let my dreams die,' Solene said. 'And now it is too late.'

'It's never too late, Madame Joubert,' Clementine said, 'and your puppets are much better than Madame Delacroix's.'

'How dare you?' Paulette barked from where she was lying on the floor. 'My puppets are the best in France!'

'I'd keep quiet if I were you,' Aunt Violet snapped.

'We will need you to come to the police station to make a statement, Madame Joubert, and we will be taking Madame Delacroix into custody,' Office Dufour informed them.

Clarissa looked at her watch and gasped. 'And we need to get back to the hotel. The car is coming to collect us in ten minutes!'

'Do not worry – he can get the bags at the hotel and come here to pick you up,' said Camille, whipping out her phone.

The family and friends walked back outside.

Clementine turned to Sophie. 'So we're really going this time,' she said sadly, and the two friends hugged.

Etienne Rousseau looked at Clementine. '*Merci*, *ma chérie*,' the man said, his eyes twinkling.

'*Merci*, Monsieur Rousseau,' the child replied. 'I never would have found Lavender if it weren't for you.'

'And I would never have found my dear friend if it were not for you.' He blew Clementine a kiss, which she caught and blew right back.

Clementine smiled. 'Just like a missing piece of a puzzle.'

'*Au revoir*, Clementine and sweet little Lavender,' Solene said softly. She waved goodbye and left arm in arm with Etienne.

Clementine felt something tickle her nose. She looked up and could hardly believe her eyes. 'It's snowing!' she gasped, and stuck out her tongue to catch some flakes.

'Goodness, that has to be the most exciting end to a holiday I've ever had,' Uncle Digby said. 'Although I think I'll need another one after all that rushing about.'

'Indeed,' Aunt Violet sniffed. 'Perhaps Clarissa can win us an island getaway.'

'So you're going on holidays together, just the two of you?' Clementine said. She waggled her eyebrows, beaming as the soft snow caught in her lashes.

Aunt Violet rolled her eyes. 'Oh, don't be ridiculous, Clementine. We'd kill each other in a minute.'

Uncle Digby grinned and the others laughed.

'You know, I really don't think that's true,' Clementine said, and Lavender squealed as if to agree.

# CAST OF CHARACTERS

| | |
|---|---|
| Clementine Rose Appleby | Six-year-old daughter of Lady Clarissa |
| Lavender | Clementine's teacup pig |
| Lady Clarissa Appleby | Clementine's mother and the owner of Penberthy House |
| Digby Pertwhistle | Butler at Penberthy House |
| Aunt Violet Appleby | Clementine's grandfather's sister |
| Drew Barnsley | Clarissa's fiancé |

| | |
|---|---|
| Will Barnsley | Drew's seven-year-old son and Clementine's friend |

## Old and new friends

| | |
|---|---|
| Pierre Rousseau | Owner of Pierre's Patisserie in Highton Mill |
| Odette Rousseau | Pierre's wife and Sophie's mother |
| Sophie Rousseau | Clementine's best friend |
| Jules Rousseau | Sophie's eight-year-old brother |
| Etienne Rousseau | Pierre's father |
| Hortense | Etienne's cranky cat |
| Emmanuelle | Etienne's apprentice |
| Camille Crabbe | Co-owner of l'Hôtel Lulu |
| Henri Crabbe | Co-owner of l'Hôtel Lulu and Madame Crabbe's husband |
| Lulu | Henri's precious dachshund |
| Paulette Delacroix | Famous French puppeteer |
| Madame Joubert | Etienne's neighbour |

# LIST OF FRENCH WORDS

| | |
|---|---|
| *au revoir* | goodbye |
| *bonjour* | hello |
| *chocolat chaud* | hot chocolate |
| *cochon* | pig |
| *comme ci, comme ça* | so-so |
| *délicieux* | delicious |
| *de rien* | you're welcome |
| *entrez* | come in |
| *grand-père* | grandpa |
| *hôtel* | hotel |
| *incroyable* | incredible |

| | |
|---|---|
| *ma chérie* | my sweetheart (f.) |
| *madame* | madam |
| *magnifique* | magnificent |
| *mama* | mother |
| *merci* | thank you |
| *mini cochon* | teacup pig |
| *monsieur* | mister |
| *non* | no |
| *oui* | yes |
| *papa* | father |
| *poisson* | fish |
| *porcelet* | piglet |
| *privé* | private |
| *sacré bleu* | darn it |
| *zut alors* | shucks |

# ABOUT
# THE AUTHOR

Jacqueline Harvey taught for many years in girls' boarding schools. She is the author of the bestselling Alice-Miranda series and the Clementine Rose series, and was awarded Honour Book in the 2006 Australian CBC Awards for her picture book *The Sound of the Sea*. She now writes full-time and is working on more Alice-Miranda and Clementine Rose adventures.

**www.jacquelineharvey.com.au**

JACQUELINE
SUPPORTS

Jacqueline Harvey is a passionate educator who enjoys sharing her love of reading and writing with children and adults alike. She is an ambassador for Dymocks Children's Charities and Room to Read. Find out more at www.dcc.gofundraise.com.au and www.roomtoread.org/australia.